Happy Ever After

For Bethan
S.W.

ORCHARD BOOKS
338 Euston Road, London NW1 3BH
Orchard Books Australia
Hachette Children's Books
Level 17/207, Kent Street, Sydney, NSW 2000
ISBN 1 84362 524 5 (hardback)
ISBN 1 84362 532 6 (paperback)
First published in Great Britain in 2005
First paperback publication in 2006
Text © Tony Bradman 2005 Illustrations © Sarah Warburton 2005
1 3 5 7 9 10 8 6 4 2 (hardback)
1 3 5 7 9 10 8 6 4 2 (paperback)
The text paper this book is printed on is certified by the Forest
Stewardship Council (FSC). FSC products with percentage claims
meet environmental requirements to be ancient-forest friendly.
The printer Cox & Wyman holds FSC chain of custody TT-COC-2063.
Printed in Great Britain by Cox & Wyman, CPI Group.

Tony Bradman

Happy Ever After

JACK'S
BEAN SNACKS

Illustrated by Sarah Warburton

ORCHARD BOOKS

"Come on, Jack," said Mum. "Up the stairs and into your pyjamas, please. It's time for your beddy-byes. And don't forget to brush your teeth."

"But it's only seven o'clock!" spluttered
Jack. "And do you have to talk to me
like that, Mum? I am NOT a little boy
any more."

"Well, you are to me," said Mum.
"Now up those stairs..."

"But I'm a hero, Mum," said Jack. "I climbed the beanstalk...

...outwitted the terrifying giant...

...and got my picture in all the newspapers, remember?"

"How could I forget?" Mum sighed. "It could have been a disaster! You never think things through, Jack. I sent you to sell poor old Daisy the cow because we had no money, and all you came home with was a few beans."

"*Magic* beans," said Jack. "And everything worked out OK, didn't it? I brought you back a bag of gold, and a hen that lays golden eggs."

"Huh! The gold lasted a week, and that hen only lays an egg when she feels like it, which is about once a month," Mum snorted.

"So we're not as rich as everyone in the forest seems to think," she went on. "I don't get time to laze around watching TV, anyway. Not like some people I could mention."

"You liked the Singing Harp, though, didn't you?" Jack muttered.

"Oh yes," said Mum. "Till I discovered it sings the same song over and over again!

"Now if you're not upstairs by the time I count to five..."

"OK, OK, I'm going," Jack grumbled.

Later, Mum came up to check that Jack had brushed his teeth, and to give him a night-night kiss.

Jack lay in bed, unable to sleep, wondering what he could do to make Mum treat him differently.

He remembered what she'd said about not having time to laze around, and suddenly he felt guilty. Perhaps if he helped her more...

In the morning, when Jack came down to breakfast...

"There just aren't enough hours in the day..." Mum was muttering to herself. "How can I go to the supermarket and get the washing done?"

"Don't worry, Mum," said Jack. "I'll do the shopping for you."

"Oh no, I don't think so," Mum said, shaking her head. "What's brought this on, anyway?"

"I'd just like to help you," said Jack, giving her a big smile. "And couldn't you tell me what to do? I mean, it can't be that hard, can it?"

"Oh, all right, then," said Mum. "Here's the list and some money. It's more than you'll need, so I expect to see plenty of change. Come straight back from the supermarket and don't talk to strangers, OK?"

"No problem, Mum," said Jack. "You can trust me."

Jack set off, and soon arrived at the forest superstore. He grabbed a trolley and quickly made his way to the fruit and vegetable section.

Mr and Mrs Goldilocks were already there, glumly examining the produce.

"You know, I'm bored with eating the same things the whole time..." said Mr Goldilocks. "They don't have much variety here, do they?"

Jack looked round. He had to agree.
So he moved on to the next section
without picking up anything, even
though fruit and vegetables were the
first items on Mum's list.

He scanned the rest of the list and
frowned.

None of it was very exciting. What Mum needed was a little treat to cheer her up. A couple of big tubs of Double Choc Chip ice cream should do the trick.

Half an hour later, Jack's trolley was filled to overflowing with treats of all kinds - ice cream, sweets, chocolate bars, crisps of every flavour, cookies and cakes and bottles of fizzy drink.

He had spent all of the money, and he hadn't bought anything that was on Mum's list. And when he got home, Mum was very very cross with him.

"Oh Jack, what have you done?" she moaned. Jack's smile vanished. "We can't live on stuff like this! Besides, I'm trying to lose weight."

"I was only trying to cheer you up, Mum," Jack muttered.

"Well, you've done exactly the opposite," said Mum. "I'll have to do the shopping all over again tomorrow, and we really can't afford to waste money. So you can go straight to bed without any supper."

That evening, Jack lay in bed, unable to sleep, wondering what he should do. Everything seemed to come back to money. Mum was always fretting about not having enough.

Maybe he should go on another exciting adventure, he thought, or even lots of adventures, and win enough treasure to keep them in luxury for the rest of their lives...

The next morning, Jack came downstairs, ate his breakfast and behaved as normal. He was waiting for Mum to leave for the supermarket.

"Bye, Jack," said Mum at last. "Be a good boy while I'm out, OK?"

"What makes you think I'd be anything else?" said Jack, smiling.

Mum rolled her eyes. And as soon as she'd gone, Jack grabbed the hen that laid the golden eggs and ran off. He searched high and low for someone who could sell him more magic beans.

At last a man listened to him, and gave him a strange look. The man asked about the hen, then smiled. "Magic beans?" he said. "No problem, kid. I've got loads!"

So Jack swapped the hen for a
hundred beans. He was very pleased,
and had them planted well before Mum
got back from the supermarket.

That evening, to Mum's surprise, Jack sent himself to bed early. In the morning, he dashed downstairs. Mum was looking out of the window.

"There you go, Mum," said Jack, proudly. "All our problems are solved! Well, they will be as soon as I've climbed a few of those huge beanstalks, outwitted some more giants, and won loads of treasure..."

"Huge beanstalks?" said Mum, puzzled. "All I see is a garden full of ordinary bean plants. Where did they come from? And where's the hen?"

"Oh no, I don't believe it!" moaned
Jack, looking out of the window too.
"I've been tricked! They should be an
awful lot bigger than that…"

Of course, Mum was more cross with him than ever when he told her what he'd done. Now the hen was gone they had nothing at all to live on.

"I despair of you, Jack!" Mum said at last. "I know you're trying to help, but when are you going to learn to think before you do anything?"

And with that, Mum went off to lie down in a darkened room.

Jack trudged into the garden. He was
desperate to make Mum change her
mind about him. If only he hadn't
swapped the hen for these titchy bean
plants, he thought, and kicked one of
them very hard.

A shower of beans pattered onto the
ground - and suddenly Jack remembered
what Mr Goldilocks had said at the
superstore.

Not enough variety, eh? Well, maybe
they'd like to sell...beans! He hadn't seen
any of them at the superstore. Jack ran
off to fetch a basket...

Jack did sell his beans to the Forest Superstore. He was very tempted to blow the profits on a present for Mum, but he didn't. He thought about what she'd said – and he bought a lot more beans instead...

Within a few years, Jack's hundred beanstalks had made him the richest farmer in the forest. He was brilliant at coming up with ideas for new products, and outwitting the competition.

His picture was in the papers all the time. And he always thought before he did anything now. So Mum never, ever had to worry about money again.

She was very proud of him. "That's my son!" she would say to all the neighbours, and she let him stay up as late as he wanted. Well, almost...

And so amazingly enough, Jack and his Mum really did live...
HAPPILY EVER AFTER!

Happy Ever After

Written by Tony Bradman
Illustrated by Sarah Warburton

These books are available from all good bookshops, or can be ordered direct
from the publisher: Orchard Books, PO BOX 29, Douglas IM99 1BQ.
Credit card orders please telephone 01624 836000 or fax 01624 837033 or
visit our Internet site: www.wattspub.co.uk or
e-mail: bookshop@enterprise.net for details.

To order please quote title, author and ISBN and your full name and
address. Cheques and postal orders should be made payable to 'Bookpost
plc.' Postage and packing is FREE within the UK
(overseas customers should add £1.00 per book).

Prices and availability are subject to change.